JEN BREACH

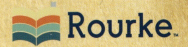

ROURKE'S SCHOOL to HOME CONNECTIONS
BEFORE AND DURING READING ACTIVITIES

Before Reading: *Building Background Knowledge and Vocabulary*

Building background knowledge can help children process new information and build upon what they already know. Before reading a book, it is important to tap into what children already know about the topic. This will help them develop their vocabulary and increase their reading comprehension.

Questions and Activities to Build Background Knowledge:

1. Look at the front cover of the book and read the title. What do you think this book will be about?
2. What do you already know about this topic?
3. Take a book walk and skim the pages. Look at the table of contents, photographs, captions, and bold words. Did these text features give you any information or predictions about what you will read in this book?

Vocabulary: *Vocabulary Is Key to Reading Comprehension*

Use the following directions to prompt a conversation about each word:
- Read the vocabulary words.
- What comes to mind when you see each word?
- What do you think each word means?

Vocabulary Words:
- adapted
- colonist
- foraged
- immigrant
- regional
- techniques

During Reading: *Reading for Meaning and Understanding*

To achieve deep comprehension of a book, children are encouraged to use close reading strategies. During reading, it is important to have children stop and make connections. These connections result in deeper analysis and understanding of a book.

Close Reading a Text

During reading, have children stop and talk about the following:
- Any confusing parts
- Any unknown words
- Text-to-text, text-to-self, text-to-world connections
- The main idea in each chapter or heading

Encourage children to use context clues to determine the meaning of any unknown words. These strategies will help children learn to analyze the text more thoroughly as they read.

When you are finished reading this book, turn to the next-to-last page for **After-Reading Questions** and an **Activity**.

TABLE OF CONTENTS

American Melting Pots 4

Modern American (?) Foods 8

Recipe: How to Cook Succotash 30

Index 31

After-Reading Questions 31

Activity 31

About the Author 32

American food is a mix of native, **colonist**, and **immigrant** food traditions.

American Indians grew crops called the "Three Sisters": corn, beans, and squash. They also fished, hunted, and trapped meat or traded for it, and **foraged** for wild greens, wild rice, nuts, and fruits like cranberries.

colonist (KAH-luh-nist): a person who lives in a colony or who helps establish a colony

immigrant (IM-i-gruhnt): someone who moves from one country to another and settles there

foraged (FOR-ijd): to have gone in search of food

THE LONG WAY AROUND FOR A TOMATO

Tomatoes, potatoes, peanuts, and chocolate came to North America with European immigrants. But these foods were brought to Europe from South America by Spanish and Portuguese colonists. That's taking the long way around!

Succotash, an American Indian stew of corn and beans, was shared with colonists in the 17th century. It is still an all-American dish to this day.

European explorers, traders, and colonists introduced American Indians to cows, goats, sheep, pigs, stone fruit, apples, cantaloupe, lemons, wheat, flour, potatoes, tomatoes, chili peppers, pickles, and sugar.

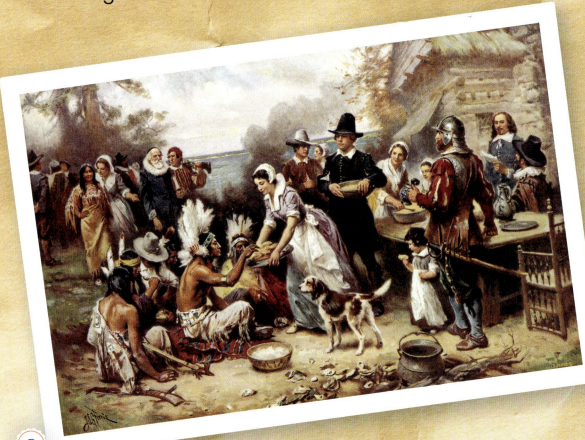

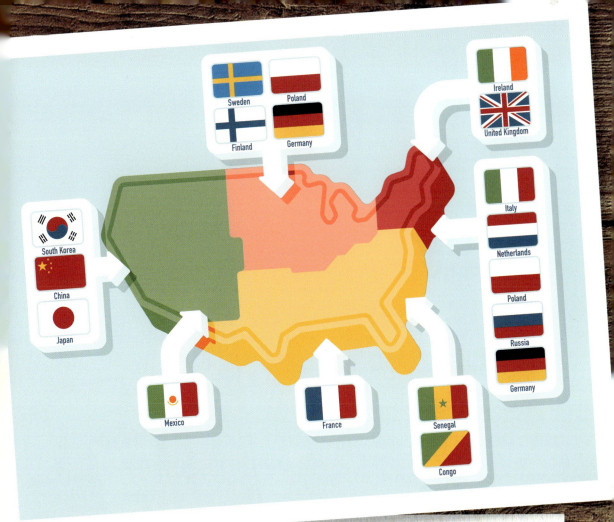

WHO SETTLED WHERE, AND WHAT DID THEY BRING?

British colonists and Irish immigrants in New England: baked pies, potatoes, wheat, oats, animals for meat and dairy
Dutch colonists in New York City: fried dough, cabbage, pretzels
French colonists in Louisiana: roux-based sauces
West African enslaved people in the South: rice, okra, watermelon
German and Polish immigrants in the Midwest: sausages, pierogies, sauerkraut
Swedish and Finnish immigrants in the Midwest: pancakes, butter-heavy baking, sweet doughs
Jewish immigrants in New York City: smoked fish and meats, deli-style sandwiches
Italian immigrants in New York City: pizza, pasta
Mexican immigrants in the Southwest: tacos, mole, enchiladas, and more
Asian immigrants in California: stir-fry, noodles, dumplings, tangerines

AMERICAN MELTING POTS

MODERN AMERICAN(?) FOODS

PIZZA
(IS FROM ITALY!)

Pizza was invented in Italy before 997 A.D. It came to the United States with Italian immigrants between 1880 and 1920. These immigrants settled in cities like Detroit, Chicago, New York City, and New Haven, Connecticut. Each place **adapted** its own signature pie.

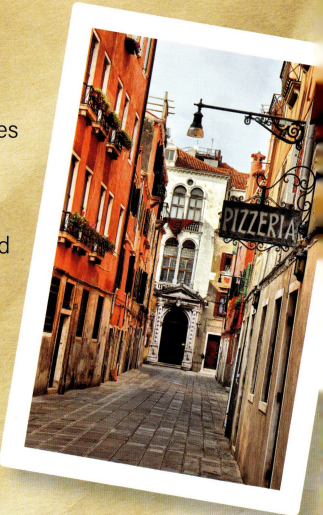

adapted (uh-DAPT-ed): made to work in a different way or for a different purpose

MODERN AMERICAN(?) FOODS

A SLICE OR A SQUARE?

Detroit: rectangular pies, slices are called "squares," have a thick but light crust with crispy cheese
Chicago: deep, round pies, layers of crust, cheese, and toppings, tomato sauce on top
New Haven, CT: called "apizza," superthin, charred, crispy crust
New York City: slices big enough to fold (and NEVER eaten with a knife and fork)

SANDWICHES
(ARE FROM ENGLAND)

Sandwiches were invented in 1762 by the unnamed cook of the Earl of Sandwich, a British noble. In the United States, sandwiches were popular with dockworkers from the 1920s to 1960s. Most **regional** differences are named after the slang terms for dockworkers.

regional (REE-juhn-uhl): related or limited to a particular geographical area

Americans eat nearly 300 million sandwiches a day. That's almost one per person!

MODERN AMERICAN(?) FOODS

WHAT'S IN A (SANDWICH) NAME?

Midwest, California, or New England: grinder or sub
New York and New Jersey: hero
Delaware and parts of the Midwest: sub
Louisiana: po'boy
Mid-Atlantic: hoagie
Maine: Italian sandwich (even though it's one hundred percent American!)

CHILI IS ALL-AMERICAN
(BY WAY OF SPANISH NORTH AFRICA)

In the 1860s, San Antonio was the biggest city in Texas. "Chili Queens" sold bowls of cheap and nourishing chili in the city square from colorful carts. The Chili Queens were immigrants from a Spanish colony in the Canary Islands, off the coast of North Africa. Their chili was so popular that the 1893 Chicago World's Fair included a San Antonio Chili Stand! From there, it spread to the rest of the United States, with many regional differences that made use of local, easy-to-access ingredients.

MODERN AMERICAN(?) FOODS

THE TRADITIONAL FAMILY RECIPE

Texas: beef chunks in a tomato stew
New Mexico: pork chunks with poblanos and tomatillos in a green sauce
the Midwest: tomato-based stew with ground beef and beans
Cincinnati, OH: piled on spaghetti or on a hot dog, topped with a mound of cheddar, maybe onions and beans
Springfield, Il: any ground meat, beans, no tomatoes
Missouri: ground beef served dry, not soupy
Kansas City, KS: dryish and made with beans and burnt ends of barbecue pork and beef

There are two things all chili recipes have in common—cumin and chili peppers!

HOT DOGS
(ARE ACTUALLY FROM GERMANY)

German and Polish immigrants brought their national sausages to the United States in the mid-1800s. Street food vendors found that the easiest way to serve a sausage was in a bun, and it could be dressed up in all sorts of ways beyond ketchup, mustard, and relish. What do you like on your hot dog?

TASTY TOPPINGS

Chicago: raw onion, sweet relish, mustard, a pickle spear, pickled peppers, slices of fresh tomato—NO KETCHUP!
Southern U.S.: chili, creamy coleslaw, raw onion
Missouri: melted Swiss cheese and tangy sauerkraut
Arizona: bacon, raw onion, chopped tomato, pinto beans, avocado, jalapeños
Seattle: cream cheese, jalapeños, grilled onion and cabbage, BBQ sauce, Sriracha, or salsa
Colorado: green chili sauce, sour cream, raw red onion
New Jersey: baked potato!
Texas: melted cheddar and pickled jalapeños

BARBECUE
(IS FROM THE CARIBBEAN)

Barbecue was brought to the United States from the Caribbean by Spanish and British colonists in the early 1700s. American barbecue uses some **techniques** that American Indians use for smoking fish and meat.

Regional styles developed wherever barbecue went, usually based on the cheapest meat available and the local tastes.

techniques (tek-NEEKZ): methods or ways of doing something that require skill

KANSAS CITY

TEXAS

MEMPHIS, TN

MODERN AMERICAN(?) FOODS

AS LONG AS IT'S COOKED LOW AND SLOW . . .

Carolinas: a whole pig cooked "wet" in a tangy vinegar-based sauce
Memphis, TN: dry-rubbed pulled pork with a sweet sauce of molasses and tomatoes
Texas: beef brisket (a Jewish tradition) with sauce that is a little sweet, a little spicy, and a little tangy
Kansas City: any meat smothered in thick, sweet sauce

Barbecue has fiercely regional flavors, but the sides know no state boundaries. You can't go wrong with potato salad (originally from Germany), a cabbage slaw (from the Netherlands), cornbread, and baked beans (both American Indian recipes). And don't forget a Polish dill pickle!

HOW TO COOK SUCCOTASH

INGREDIENTS

- 2 tablespoons olive oil
- ½ white onion, minced
- 4 cups frozen corn
- 2 cups frozen lima beans
- 1 bell pepper or poblano, finely diced
- 1 pint cherry tomatoes, halved
- 1 teaspoon garlic powder
- ½ teaspoon smoked paprika
- ½ teaspoon ground sage
- 1 teaspoon kosher salt
- freshly ground black pepper (to taste)
- 1 tablespoon salted butter (or olive oil)
- 2 tablespoons finely chopped fresh parsley, cilantro, scallions, or a mix

INSTRUCTIONS

1. Heat the olive oil in a large skillet over medium-high heat. Add the onion and cook for 2 minutes, until translucent.
2. Add the corn, beans, red pepper, tomatoes, garlic powder, smoked paprika, sage, salt, and black pepper. Cook, stirring occasionally, until all vegetables are tender and nearly cooked, about 5 to 6 minutes.
3. Stir in the salted butter and herbs. Cook 1 minute more, until the butter is melted. Taste and add additional salt if desired. Serve warm.

INDEX

American Indian(s) 4, 6, 24, 28
barbecue 18, 24, 28
chili 6, 16, 19, 22
hot dog(s) 18, 20
local 16, 24
pizza 7, 8, 10
sandwich(es) 7, 12, 13, 14, 15

AFTER-READING QUESTIONS

1. What is the difference between Memphis-style and Texas-style barbecue?
2. Immigrants from which countries brought hot dogs to the United States?
3. In which American city was chili invented?
4. What do New Yorkers call a sandwich?
5. What does the author mean by "the sides know no state boundaries" on page 28?

ACTIVITY

Pick three dishes not in this book that you enjoy and eat often. Good examples might be spaghetti and meatballs or chicken pot pie. Think about the ingredients in each dish. Write down where you think each dish was invented. Then do some research to find out if you are right!

ABOUT THE AUTHOR

Jen Breach (pronouns: they/them) is queer and nonbinary. Jen grew up in a tiny town in rural Australia with three older brothers, two parents, and one pet duck. Jen has worked as an archaeologist, a librarian, an editor, a florist, a barista, a bagel-baker, a code-breaker, a ticket-taker, and a trouble-maker. The best job they ever had was as a writer, which they do now in Philadelphia, Pennsylvania. Jen likes New York pizza, Philadelphia hoagies, New Mexican chili, Wisconsin brats, and every single kind of BBQ there is.

© 2023 Rourke Educational Media

All rights reserved. No part of this book may be reproduced or utilized in any form or by any means, electronic or mechanical including photocopying, recording, or by any information storage and retrieval system without permission in writing from the publisher.

www.rourkebooks.com

PHOTO CREDITS: Cover: Brent Hofacker/ Shutterstock.com; pages 4- 5: Rasmus S/ Shutterstock.com; page 5: Everett Collection/ Shutterstock.com; page 6: Everett Collection/ Shutterstock.com; page 8: JeniFoto/ Shutterstock.com; page 9: LOGAN WEAVER on Unsplash; page 10: Supitcha McAdam/ Shutterstock.com; page 10: Ranta Images/ Shutterstock.com; page 11: Brent Hofacker/ Shutterstock.com; page 11: Jordan Nix on Unsplash; page 12: Pictore/ Getty Images; page 13: Dean Drobot/ Shutterstock.com; page 14: Brent Hofacker/ Shutterstock.com; page 15: TonelsonProductions/ Shutterstock.com; page 16: Everett Collection/ Shutterstock.com; page 17: gontabunta/ Shutterstock.com; page 17: StockImageFactory.com/ Shutterstock.com; page 18: Keith Mecklem/ Shutterstock.com; page 18: Brent Hofacker/ Shutterstock.com; page 18: Marie Sonmez Photography/ Shutterstock.com; page 19: GMVozd/ Getty Images; page 20: Tom Sweeney/Minneapolis Star Tribune/ZUMAPRESS.com; page 21: Detroit Publishing Company; page 21: CRAIG PORTER/KRT/Newscom; page 23: Brent Hofacker/ Shutterstock.com; page 23: Brent Hofacker/ Shutterstock.com; page 24: Horace Bradley/ Wikimedia Commons; page 24: TonelsonProductions/ Shutterstock.com; page 26: Marie Sonmez Photography/ Shutterstock.com; page 26: Foodio/ Shutterstock.com; page 26: KarepaStock/ Shutterstock.com; page 27: Joshua Resnick/ Shutterstock.com; page 28: praetorianphoto/ Getty Images; page 29: Elena Veselova/ Shutterstock.com; page 30: Brent Hofacker/ Shutterstock.com: Pages: 7, 17, 20-21, 24-25, 28-29: Ales Krivec on Unsplash; Pages: 5, 7, 9-10, 12, 14, 18, 22, 25, 27, 30-32: Lana Veshta/ Shutterstock.com; pages: 1, 3-4, 6, 8, 10-12, 14-16, 18-20, 22-24, 26-28, 30-32: Nas photo/ Shutterstock.com.

Edited by: Catherine Malaski
Cover and interior design by: Max Porter

Library of Congress PCN Data

Just What Is American Food, Anyway? / Jen Breach
(Food Tour)
ISBN 978-1-73165-272-0 (hard cover)(alk. paper)
ISBN 978-1-73165-235-5 (soft cover)
ISBN 978-1-73165-302-4 (e-book)
ISBN 978-1-73165-332-1 (e-pub)
Library of Congress Control Number: 2021952193

Rourke Educational Media
Printed in the United States of America
01-2412211937